The Kid Coach

The Kid Coach

by Fred Bowen

Illustrated by
Ann Barrow

PEACHTREE
ATLANTA

Other books by Fred Bowen

T. J.'s SECRET PITCH
THE GOLDEN GLOVE
PLAYOFF DREAMS
FULL COURT FEVER
OFF THE RIM
THE FINAL CUT
ON THE LINE
WINNERS TAKE ALL

A Peachtree Junior Publication

Published by
PEACHTREE PUBLISHERS, LTD.
1700 Chattahoochee Avenue
Atlanta, Georgia 30318-2112

www.peachtree-online.com

Text ©1996 by Fred Bowen
Illustrations © 1996 by Ann Barrow

Lou Boudreau photo courtesy of the National Baseball Hall of Fame Library, Cooperstown, NY.

Jacket illustration by Ann G. Barrow
Book design by Loraine M. Balcsik
Composition by Dana Celentano

Manufactured in the United States of America
10 9 8 7 6 5

Library of Congress Cataloging-in-Publication Data

Bowen, Fred.
      The kid coach / Fred Bowen ; illustrated by Ann Barrow.
            p. cm. — (Allstar sportstory)Summary: When they lose their coach, Scott and his teammates decide that he should try his hand at coaching, but it takes teamwork and the efforts of a player they call "Brain" to produce a winning season.
      ISBN 1-56145-140-1 (pbk.)
      [1. Baseball—Fiction. 2. Coaching (Athletics)—Fiction.]
      I. Barrow, Ann, ill. II. Title. III. Series: Bowen, Fred. Allstar sportstory.
PZ7.B6724Ki   1997
      [Fic]—dc21   96-45923
                                                                              CIP
                                                                              AC

To all the kids I have coached
at Woodlin Elementary School.

ONE

"What do you want to do?"

Scott Hudson watched the spring rain splash tiny rivers on the living room window.

"I don't know," Scott said. "What do you want to do?"

Drew Moyers, Scott's best friend and Tigers teammate, walked across the room and joined Scott at the window.

"We sure aren't going to have baseball practice today," he said.

Scott shrugged. "What does it matter?" he asked. "Coach Skelly would have been late anyway."

"What's his story?" Drew asked. "He's always late for practice."

Scott searched the skies for a break in the clouds. The sky stayed steely gray. "I don't know," he said. "My dad says he's starting a new business or something."

"Remember when his beeper went off during practice and he ran to the phone like his pants were on fire?" Drew laughed.

Scott laughed too, but his smile quickly melted into a frown. "He better be there when we scrimmage the Red Sox," he said.

"Yeah, but I hope Mr. Skelly doesn't play Max at third. Max can't throw," Drew said. "I think Fran could make the throw from third."

Just then, Scott saw a yellow-hooded figure dash across the front yard. "Hey, guess who's here?" called Scott as he went to open the door. "It's Fran."

Mary Frances McDermott, Scott's next-door neighbor and teammate, stepped in and shook the rain off her coat. "Hey, guys, what are you doing?"

"Hey, Fran, can you make the throw from third?" Drew asked.

"Sure, no sweat," Fran said. "Why? Do you think that girls can't throw?" she asked, looking straight at Drew.

"No, gimme a break," said Drew, holding up his hands. "We think you should be playing third instead of Max."

"So do I. But we're not coaches. We're just players," Fran replied.

"Hey! Let's make up a lineup!" shouted Scott. "You know, like who we would start if we were coaching."

"Well, there's nothing else to do," Drew shrugged.

"Yeah, let's do it," said Fran.

Scott found a piece of paper and a pencil and sat down in front of the coffee table with his legs underneath him. His two friends sat at either end of the table leaning toward Scott.

"Let's start with pitcher," Scott suggested.

"That's a cinch," Drew said. "You and me pitch. When I pitch, you play shortstop. When you pitch, I'll play shortstop." The boys exchanged high fives before Scott wrote down their names.

"Put Danny at catcher," Fran said.

"Yeah, that's good," Scott said. "And what about Brendan in the outfield?"

"Just so long as he's not near a snack machine," said Drew. "Boy, does he like to eat!"

"Okay. How about Max at first?" Scott asked.

"Nah," said Drew. "Nick's taller. He makes a better target."

Fran nodded and Scott wrote it down. The

"Let's start with pitcher."

three friends went through the Tigers roster matching players with positions.

"We forgot Benny," Fran said. "We gotta put him someplace."

"Benny the Brain!" Drew howled. "That computer nerd! He stinks!"

"He's not bad," Fran protested. "He's a pretty fast runner."

"He runs goofy," Drew said. "It's like he borrowed someone else's legs."

"You don't like him because he's so much better at math than you are," Fran said.

"I'm better at math than he is at baseball," Drew snapped back. "At least I get Cs in math. The Brain wouldn't get a D in baseball."

"Let's get back to the lineup, guys," Scott said, pointing to the paper. "We gotta play Benny somewhere. What about someplace in the outfield?"

"Outfield?!" Drew blurted. "We oughta play him someplace in *cyberfield*."

Scott laughed and wrote it down.

"Let's take a look at what we got," Fran said. The three teammates studied the lineup.

TIGERS

Starters

P	Scott/Drew
C	Danny Perlstein
1B	Nicholas Chu
2B	Maggie Ferris
SS	Drew/Scott
3B	Fran
LF	Max Stevenson
CF	Peter Martinez
RF	Sam Finch

Reserves

Eric Jaworski	infield
Brendan Lynch	outfield
Michael Stamm	outfield
Benny the Brain	cyberfield

"It looks pretty good," Fran said.

"We're better coaches than Mr. Skelly," Drew said.

Scott laughed, folded the paper, and stuffed it in his pocket. He walked backed to the window, desperately looking for some blue sky.

It was still raining.

TWO

Scott stood in center field with his hands on his hips, feeling as if he were watching a whole year of baseball go down the drain. It was time for the Tigers-Red Sox scrimmage and Mr. Skelly was nowhere in sight.

The Red Sox were warming up on the sidelines, firing baseballs back and forth. The Tigers looked like a bunch of kids with nothing to do. Some of the kids played a lazy game of catch while others just hung around the dugout.

Fran and Drew walked over to Scott.

"Where's Mr. Skelly?" Fran asked.

Scott looked at the ground and shook his head. "Who knows," he muttered.

"Well, he better get here soon," Drew said, pointing to the Tigers bench. "Brendan's gonna finish off that whole bag of potato chips all by himself."

"Man, look at Benny!" Scott said. "He's reading a book on the bench! I'll bet the Red Sox are real impressed with us."

Scott slammed his glove down on the outfield grass and shoved his hands into his pockets. In his right pocket, he felt a crumpled piece of paper.

"Hey!" he said, pulling the paper from his pocket and holding it up to show Fran and Drew. It was the Tigers lineup they had dreamed up together. "Why don't we use this lineup for the scrimmage?"

"I don't know," Drew said. "We're not really coaches. We were just fooling around."

"It's worth a try," Fran said, shrugging her shoulders. "I just want to play."

Scott took the paper and marched up to Mr. Robinson, a tall man with a clipboard. He was the Red Sox coach.

"Hi, Mr. Robinson."

"Hi, Scottie. Where's Mr. Skelly?"

"I don't know. He's been late a lot this year. But we're ready to play."

Mr. Robinson looked at the Tigers milling around the field. "Are you sure?" he asked.

Scott nodded and held up the wrinkled piece

of paper. "We've got a lineup and everything, see?"

"All right." Mr. Robinson smiled. "It's just a scrimmage. I'll call balls and strikes from behind the mound. You guys want first ups?"

"No, we'll take the field," Scott said. He called out to Drew and Fran, "Come on, we got a scrimmage to play!"

Drew and Fran smiled at each other and ran to the Tigers bench.

"Everybody in!" shouted Scott.

The Tigers gathered around Scott. "Where's Mr. Skelly?" Nick asked.

"I don't know, but we've got a lineup, so listen up."

"Can I play infield?" Peter asked.

"Keep quiet and listen to Scott," Drew said. "And put those chips down, Brendan!"

Brendan looked surprised. He put the bag of chips down on the bench and wiped his mouth with his T-shirt.

"All right, we're in the field first," Scott called out. "Drew's gonna pitch. Danny's behind the plate. I'm playing short. Fran's at third. Maggie's at second and Nick's at first. Max, you're gonna start in left. Pete, you're in center. Sam, why don't you start in right.

I'll get everybody else in later. Let's go!"

The Tigers hustled onto the field. Drew took a few warm-up pitches and Mr. Robinson called, "Play ball!"

The leadoff Red Sox batter stepped to the plate and knocked a hard grounder to shortstop. Scott scooted over a few steps to his left, gathered in the grounder, and threw to first.

"Out," Mr. Robinson called.

"All right!"

"Nice play, Scott!"

Scott grinned. The Tigers were finally playing some baseball!

The second Red Sox batter smacked a hard single to center field and then the tall, strong Red Sox slugger, Eddie Wilson, stepped to the plate. "Move back!" Scott called out to his outfielders.

It didn't matter. Eddie belted the second pitch far out into right field. Scott gave a small admiring whistle as the ball sailed high over the right-field fence for a two-run homer.

"Shake it off, Drew!" Scott shouted from shortstop. "It's just a scrimmage."

The game continued for a few more innings. The Tigers got a couple of runs but the Red Sox pushed ahead when Eddie Wilson smacked a two-run double down the right-field line.

Scott tried to give everyone a chance to play. Before the final inning, he called down the bench, "Hey, Benny, you want to play right field?"

"Sure," Benny said.

"Then put the book down and grab your glove," Drew said. "What's that book about anyway?"

"Baseball."

"Well, it's time to *play* baseball, not just read about it," Drew said. "Let's go."

The Red Sox added another run in the final inning. The Tigers could not come back as Benny, Eric, and Brendan all struck out to end the scrimmage.

Despite the loss, the Tigers were upbeat as they gathered their baseball gear and headed home. Scott and Fran rode their bikes side by side along a dirt path that cut through an open field. "You did a pretty good job, Coach," Fran said.

"We did okay," Scott said. "At least we got

to play. Lost to the Red Sox 5–2. That's not too bad. I don't know if Mr. Skelly could have done better than that."

Fran dropped back into single file as the two friends turned onto a busy street.

"Mr. Skelly never did show up!" she shouted up to Scott. "I wonder what happened to him?"

THREE

Mr. Skelly's whistle cut through the cool spring air. "Bring it in," he called.

The Tigers gathered in a small circle around their coach. Some kids sat back on the soft infield grass while others knelt on their knees.

Mr. Skelly looked around the group and said, "Listen, kids, I'm sorry I missed the scrimmage. I called all your parents and I hope they explained that there was an emergency at work." Mr. Skelly took a deep breath and continued, "You've probably noticed that I've been really busy at work. And...ah...I've been thinking that I...ah...really can't coach you guys this year. I'm just not sure I could make all the games and practices."

The Tigers traded silent glances and fidgeted on the grass.

Mr. Skelly adjusted his baseball cap and

went on. "I told your parents all this, but I asked them to let me be the one to tell you guys. I also asked your parents if any of them could coach the team, but...ah...none of them wanted to, I mean, none of them could do it. They're really busy, too."

"My dad goes to Australia on business a lot," Brendan said.

"He mentioned that, Brendan," Mr. Skelly said.

"I wish he'd take Brendan with him," Drew whispered to Scott.

"Anyway, I'm going to go to a league meeting tomorrow evening to see if the board can find you a new coach," Mr. Skelly said.

"He'll probably miss the meeting," Scott mumbled under his breath to Drew.

"Don't worry," Mr. Skelly said, still addressing the whole team. "You're definitely going to get to play your first game and that's in three days. In fact, here's your schedule for the season." The Tigers all jumped up at once and tried to grab one.

"Hold on! Everybody will get one," Mr. Skelly said.

As soon as Scott got his, he sat back down on the grass and studied it.

Apr 13	1:00 P.M.	Expos
Apr 17	6:30 P.M.	Braves
Apr 20	11:00 A.M.	Cubs
Apr 23	6:30 P.M.	Yankees
Apr 27	3:00 P.M.	Red Sox
May 1	6:30 P.M.	Expos
May 4	11:00 A.M.	Braves
May 7	6:30 P.M.	Cubs
May 10	6:30 P.M.	Yankees
May 14	6:30 P.M.	Red Sox
May 18	3:00 P.M.	Expos
May 23	6:30 P.M.	Braves
May 25	1:00 P.M.	Cubs
May 29	6:30 P.M.	Yankees
June 1	3:00 P.M.	Red Sox

As Scott and his teammates looked over the schedules, Mr. Skelly continued talking. "I'll keep trying to find you a coach," he said. "But right now, let's get some practice."

Mr. Skelly clapped his hands and grabbed a bat. "Max, take third. Drew, shortstop. Scott, you're on the mound. Fran's on second, Peter's on first. Danny's catching. Everybody else is running. Let's go!"

Mr. Skelly cracked a one-hopper to Max. The third baseman bobbled the ball and could not throw to first in time to stop the speeding Maggie.

"All right, runner on first, force at second base."

Mr. Skelly sent a sharp grounder to Scott on the mound. Scott scooped up the ball then whirled around toward second base and fired. Drew was there. He snatched the ball out of the air, touched the bag with his foot, and threw to first for the second out.

"That's two!"

"Double play!"

Scott broke into a big smile on the mound and pounded his glove. "Let's get the next one!" he shouted. Then Scott heard a strange noise from home plate.

"Darn it!" Mr. Skelly muttered as he pulled his beeper off his belt.

"Scott, come here," Mr. Skelly said. "I want you to keep hitting grounders. I have to call my office. I'll be right back."

Scott felt strange standing at home plate with the bat and ball. "Okay, Fran, here comes a hot one," he called. Scott tossed the ball up and swung. But he missed the ball completely. The runners in back of Scott tried not to laugh.

Scott glanced over at Mr. Skelly talking on

16

his car phone and then smacked a grounder to second. Fran made a backhanded stab and flipped the ball to first.

"Great play!" Scott shouted.

After a few more grounders, Mr. Skelly returned and blew his whistle.

"I'm sorry, but I have to go," he said, glancing at his watch. "There's another emergency at work." Mr. Skelly pulled Scott and Drew aside and said, "You guys pick sides and play a scrimmage." Then he dashed off again and called back, "I'll let you know about the coaching situation." The Tigers watched Mr. Skelly's car spit small stones as it sped away.

Scott looked at Drew. "Well, you wanna flip a coin for first pick?" Scott asked.

"Yeah. I guess so," said Drew. "Heads I get first pick and tails you do. Fair?" asked Drew.

"Fair," said Scott and he pulled a quarter from his pocket and tossed it in the air. The quarter landed in the dirt heads up.

"I'll take Danny," Drew said.

"I got Nick."

"Fran."

"Max."

None of the Tigers moved. Finally Scott

and Drew stopped calling names.

"What are we gonna do?" asked Nick.

"About what?" Drew asked.

"About not having a coach," said Fran.

"They'll find somebody," Scott said.

"Yeah, but who?" Sam asked. "I don't want to play for just anybody. I liked Mr. Skelly."

"Well, he can't coach this year, so that's that," said Drew.

"Maybe they'll get somebody from another team or another town," Scott said, thinking out loud.

"Hey! Why don't you coach?" Nick blurted out, looking straight at Scott.

"Me?"

"Yeah, you did okay in the scrimmage."

"I don't think they would let a player coach his own team," stammered Scott.

"There's precedent for it," Benny called out from the back of the group.

"We're not looking for a president, Brain," Drew shot back. "We're looking for a coach."

"Pre-ce-dent," Benny said slowly. "It means that it has been done before."

"When?" asked Fran.

"Lots of professional teams in the first half

"Why don't you coach?"

of this century used a player as a coach," Benny said. "They called them player-coaches." Benny sounded more like a teacher than a twelve-year-old boy.

"How come you know so much about base-ball, Brain?" Drew asked. "You can't play worth anything."

"Cut it out, Drew!" Fran yelled. "He's just trying to help!"

"It sounds kind of crazy. But what do you guys think? Should I see if I can coach the team?" Scott asked, looking around at his teammates.

The circle of Tiger hats nodded.

"I'd rather have you than someone we don't know," Sam said.

"So what are we gonna do?" Scott asked.

Fran had an idea. "Why don't you and Benny go to that meeting tomorrow and ask if you can at least try it?"

"Benny can talk about that player-coach stuff," Nick said. "That might help."

"Yeah," said Drew sarcastically. "Maybe they'll make Scott the coach and Benny the pre-si-dent."

FOUR

The next evening, Scott hopped on his bike and headed for the YMCA. He locked his bike and raced up the stairs and down the hallway, his sneakers squeaking against the shiny linoleum floor.

He stopped short in front of a door marked "Youth Baseball Board Meeting." He took a deep breath and slowly turned the knob.

Inside, four men sat at a long table. Several rows of metal chairs filled the rest of the room. Scott saw Benny sitting in the back row with an opened book in his lap. Scott tiptoed up to Benny and sat down.

Mr. Skelly stood before the table with his back to Scott and Benny. He was talking.

"I've tried a bunch of people but I can't find anybody. They're either too busy or already coaching." The oldest man at the table unfolded his arms and leaned his gray head forward.

"That's Mr. Green," Benny whispered.

"We never had this problem in my day," Mr. Green said, sounding very grumpy. "We always had plenty of coaches. Assistants. Everything." He sat back and folded his arms again.

Another man, whom Scott recognized as Mr. Kirsch, spoke to Mr. Skelly. "Gee, Jack, you're putting us in a tough spot. It is only a couple of days before the first game."

"I'm sorry," Mr. Skelly said finally. "I've had some unexpected problems at the office, and things aren't going to let up for a while. I'm just too busy to coach."

The four men sat in silence. There seemed to be no solution.

Benny elbowed Scott. "What are you waiting for? Now's your chance. Say something."

Scott stood up and made his way slowly to the table. All the men were looking at him, and Mr. Skelly turned around to follow their stares. "Scott, what are you doing here?" he asked.

"Hi, Mr. Skelly. I'm here and, um, Benny's here too," said Scott, motioning to Benny to come join him, "because we had an idea that might help the coaching problem."

"Come a little closer, boys," said Mr. Kirsch. "Let's hear what you have to say."

"We...I mean, the team was thinking that since nobody could coach, maybe, you know, like, I could coach the team," Scott said.

The men shot sideways glances at each other.

"Don't you want to play on the team?" asked Mr. Kirsch.

"I want to do both, play and coach," Scott answered.

"That seems like an awful lot to do, play and coach," Mr. Kirsch said.

"Plenty of players have coached," Benny quickly added.

"What do you mean?" asked Mr. Kirsch, looking over at Benny.

"I mean a lot of great players have coached too. Ty Cobb. Rogers Hornsby. Frank Robinson and Pete Rose, too."

"They played and coached at the same time?" Mr. Kirsch asked, sounding like he didn't believe Benny.

"Yup," Benny nodded. "In 1948, Lou Boudreau played shortstop for the Cleveland Indians and coached them, too. In fact, they won the World Series that year."

Mr. Green leaned forward and he was smiling. "He was the Most Valuable Player that year. Hit around .330."

"He hit .355 with eighteen home runs and 106 runs batted in," corrected Benny.

"They had a great team," Mr. Green remembered.

"They won ninety-seven games and beat the Red Sox in a playoff," Benny observed.

"That's right!" Mr. Green almost shouted. "Boudreau used the shift on Ted Williams that game. The infielders and outfielders bunched up on the right side of the field because they knew that's where he was going to hit the ball."

Mr. Kirsch eyed Benny. "How do you know so much about this?"

"If it's in a book," Scott said, smiling, "the Brain—I mean Benny—knows it."

"The Brain?" Mr. Skelly asked.

"It's just a nickname," said Scott.

"Okay, Benny," said Mr. Kirsch. "But Lou Boudreau and most of those other player-coaches were Hall of Famers."

"I was an All-Star last year," Scott said.

"It's a little different, Scott," Mr. Skelly said. "Coaches have to run practices, figure out the lineups, make substitutions. You're only twelve years old."

"Let the kids coach the team," Mr. Green said gruffly.

"Charlie, let's be sensible," Mr. Kirsch said.

"I am being sensible," Mr. Green said, jabbing his finger at the men at the table. "Let the kids coach the team. The games are for the kids, right? So let them play. They want to try coaching? So let them try. Probably be good for them."

"Charlie," Mr. Kirsch said softly, "I'm sure we can find someone to coach their team."

"Yeah, maybe," Mr. Green said, eyeing Scott and Benny. "But tell me, where are you going to find someone who knows more about baseball than these kids?"

FIVE

"Can I see the coaches?" the umpire called from home plate.

Scott stood at the edge of the dugout holding onto the Tigers opening-day lineup. Suddenly, he was too nervous to step out.

"Go on, Scott," Fran whispered, nudging him in the back. "You're the coach, remember?"

Scott walked to home plate where the umpire and the Expos coach stood. The umpire looked at Scott.

"I want the coaches, not the captains," he said.

"I am the coach," Scott replied.

"What happened to Mr. Skelly?" the Expos coach asked.

"He's too busy, so the board said I could coach the rest of the season," Scott said.

The umpire and the Expos coach glanced at each other and traded smiles. Then the umpire and the Expos coach and Scott exchanged lineups and reviewed the ground rules. The umpire asked, "Who is the home team?"

"They are," Scott said.

"Okay, let's have a batter. Play ball."

Scott hustled back to the bench and called out to the anxious Tigers. "We're up first. Here's the batting order. Max is leading off, playing left. Nick, you're at first. Drew's pitching. Danny's catching and hitting clean-up. I'm at short. Fran, you're at third, hitting sixth. Maggie's at second. Pete's in center field. Sam, you're batting ninth and playing right. All right, let's get some hits! Get us started, Max."

The inning got off to a slow start as Max grounded out to second and Nick struck out swinging.

Drew, the Tigers best hitter, stepped into the batter's box. "Come on Drew, let's rally!"

"Be a sticker, Drew!"

The Tigers bench was on its feet as Drew hit a long fly ball to right field. The ball landed safely between two outfielders. Drew trotted to second base with a double.

"All right!"

"Way to get it started, Drew."

The Tigers had more to cheer about when Danny smacked a single up the middle. Drew raced home. The Tigers led 1–0.

Scott stepped into the batter's box next. He carefully placed his feet about shoulder-width apart, tapped the outside edge of the plate, and cocked the bat behind his right ear.

The first two pitches whistled by, wide and high. Two balls, no strikes.

Be ready, Scott thought. *He's gonna come in with one.*

Sure enough, the next pitch was right down the middle. Scott smacked the pitch past the Expos diving shortstop. That left runners on second and first, two outs.

"Come on, Fran, keep it going," Scott called breathlessly from first. "Just a bingle."

Fran delivered, her smooth swing guiding a fastball out to right field. Scott was off at the crack of the bat, dashing past second toward third. He rounded third, looking as if he were going home, but held up as the throw bounced in from right field. But Danny scored, and the Tigers led 2–0.

Rattled, the Expos hurler walked Maggie on four pitches. The bases were loaded!

Scott stood on third base, knowing a hit would break the game wide open. "Come on, Pete, bring us home!" he shouted. "Ducks on the pond." That was Scott's favorite way of saying "bases loaded."

But Peter popped up the first pitch for the third out. The score remained 2–0 with the Expos coming to bat.

"All right, let's hustle out," Scott called as the Tigers grabbed their gloves and took the field. Scott stood at the edge of the dugout and glanced down the bench. At the very end of it, Benny sat scribbling something into a notebook.

"What's he doing, his homework?" Drew asked on his way to the pitcher's mound.

"Never mind him. Let's get some outs," said Scott.

The Tigers infield was filled with chatter.

"Come on, Drew!"

"No batter, no batter."

The leadoff hitter topped a slow roller to third base. Fran took a few quick steps in, scooped up the ball, and fired to first.

"Out!"

The next Expos batter slapped a clean

single to center. One out, runner on first.

Drew turned and looked at Scott. Scott tapped his chest and said, "I'm covering second if it comes to you, Drew." The Tigers pitcher nodded and fired a fastball.

Sure enough, the Expos hitter beat a hard one-hopper back to the mound. Drew fielded it, whirled toward second, and threw. The throw met Scott at the bag. Scott caught the ball, touched the base, and threw to first. The ball smacked into Nick's glove long before the Expos runner reached the first base. The Tigers were out of the inning.

The Tigers bench was filled with cheers and backslaps.

"DP!"

"Let's keep it going!"

Scott called out the batting order: "Sam, Max, Nick, then Drew. Let's get some more!" Scott smiled as he sat at the edge of the Tigers bench. The season was off to a great start.

Scott caught the ball, touched the base,
and threw to first.

SIX

The Tigers stretched their lead to 4–1 after four innings. Danny drilled a clutch double that drove in two runs. The Tigers made some nice plays behind Drew's strong pitching.

Scott changed the lineup after the Tigers failed to score in the top of the fifth.

"Listen up," Scott called out to the Tigers bench. "Eric, you're taking Maggie's place at second. Brendan is in center, hitting eighth. Benny, you're taking Sam's place in right. We're up by three runs. Let's hang onto the lead."

But the Expos started to hit Drew's pitches hard in the bottom of the fifth. A double, a walk, and two singles scored two runs.

Scott stood at shortstop, reviewing the situation. The Tigers led 4–3, two outs in the bottom of the fifth inning. Runners on first and second.

"Big batter, Drew. Big batter."

Drew wound up and whipped the first pitch high and wide.

"Come on, Drew, throw strikes."

Drew took a deep breath and threw another pitch.

Crack!

The ball shot out like a missile to shortstop. Without even thinking, Scott dove to his left. The ball smacked hard against his outstretched glove. Scott hung on as he skidded against the infield dirt.

The Tigers still led 4–3!

The Tigers ran in from the field slapping high fives with each other.

Scott dusted himself off and called out the next inning's batters. "Benny. Max. Nick. Last ups. Let's get some runs for Drew."

Benny was in the corner of the dugout, scribbling numbers in a notebook.

"Come on, Brain. Grab a bat. You're up!" Drew shouted.

Benny stood at the edge of the dugout next to Scott. As he put on his batting helmet, he whispered, "Drew has thrown an awful lot of pitches, Scott. He's gotta be tired. You may want to take him out and let somebody else pitch the last inning."

Scott was worried about Drew's pitching, too, but he didn't want Benny to know. "Why don't you just get a hit?" Scott asked, a little too sharply. "And leave the coaching to me."

None of the Tigers could get a hit, and they went down 1-2-3 in the sixth inning. They gathered their gloves and took the field to try to hold onto their slim lead. Scott grabbed Drew by the arm. "How you doing, Drew?" he asked. "You got enough for the last inning?"

Drew jerked his arm away. "Don't worry," he said. "I'm okay."

But Drew was in trouble right away. The leadoff Expos hitter knocked a clean single right up the middle. The second batter ripped a hard line drive down the third baseline. Fran was playing near third base and snagged the hot smash. One out.

The next Expo slapped a single into right field.

"Get it in, get it in," Scott called out from shortstop, waving his glove.

Benny stopped the ball and threw it in to Scott quickly as the runner from first sprinted to the third base. Runners on first and third, one out.

Scott walked to the mound and dropped the ball into Drew's glove.

"You sure you're okay, Drew?" he asked.

"I'm fine," Drew said. "I'll get the next two guys, no sweat."

Scott trotted back to shortstop, not sure what to do. He wanted to leave his best friend in and give him a chance to win the game. But Scott was not sure that was the best thing for the team.

"Come on, Drew. Bear down."

"No batter, no batter."

The Expos batter worked the count to three balls, two strikes. Drew uncorked his best fastball. The batter swung from the heels. Strike three!

Scott held up two fingers to his teammates. "Two outs!" he shouted.

The Expos coach stepped out of the dugout and yelled to the runners on first and third, "Two outs, run on anything."

"Bear down, Drew!"

"One more, Drew, one more."

Drew got one strike on the next hitter, but

then put a pitch right down the fat part of the plate.

Crack! The Expos hitter scorched a hard liner to left center field. It hit the wall on one hop. Scott scrambled out to the outfield, shouting for Brendan to throw him the ball. "Get it in, Brendan, get it in!"

Scott knew it was too late to stop the runner on third from scoring, but hoped he could nab the runner dashing around from first base. Scott gathered in the throw and turned only to see the Expos runner cross the plate into the arms of his happy teammates.

Scott stood on the outfield grass for a long moment, holding the baseball and staring at home plate. The game was over. The Tigers trudged off the field.

Benny wrote in his notebook as the team gathered their things.

"Remember we have practice Tuesday!" Scott shouted.

"Hey, Scott," Nick said. "You gonna give out a game ball to the best player of the game like Mr. Skelly used to?"

"I'm only giving out the game ball when we win," Scott growled as he shoved the bats and batting helmets into the big brown equipment bag. Scott slung the bag over his shoulder and started the short walk home with Fran.

"It was a good game," Fran said.

"It would have been a lot better if we had won," grumbled Scott.

"We played pretty well and you did a good job coaching."

"Yeah, I guess."

When Scott got home, he plopped the bag at the bottom of the stairs and raced up to his bedroom. He found the schedule that he had placed on his desk. Next to the line that said, April 13—1 P.M.—Expos, Scott wrote: L 5–4.

He propped the schedule back up on the desk and went downstairs, slamming the bedroom door behind him.

SEVEN

Two weeks later, Scott sat on the edge of his bed lacing up his baseball spikes for another baseball practice. He glanced over to the schedule that was still on his desk. The neat rows of numbers told the sad story of the Tigers season so far.

Apr 13	1:00 P.M.	Expos	L 5-4
Apr 17	6:30 P.M.	Braves	L 3-2
Apr 20	11:00 A.M.	Cubs	L 5-3
Apr 23	6:30 P.M.	Yankees	L 4-2
Apr 27	3:00 P.M.	Red Sox	L 11-2
May 1	6:30 P.M.	Expos	
May 4	11:00 A.M.	Braves	
May 7	6:30 P.M.	Cubs	
May 10	6:30 P.M.	Yankees	
May 14	6:30 P.M.	Red Sox	
May 18	3:00 P.M.	Expos	
May 23	6:30 P.M.	Braves	
May 25	1:00 P.M.	Cubs	
May 29	6:30 P.M.	Yankees	
June 1	3:00 P.M.	Red Sox	

Scott shook his head as he remembered those games. The Tigers seemed to play just well enough to lose. They would jump off to an early lead only to lose in the later innings.

Scott jerked his glove off the dresser and headed out to practice. *The season has to turn around today*, he thought.

Practice that day was even worse. The team was only going through the motions. Batting practice was strangely quiet. The kids hardly said a word. The only sound was the crack of the bat.

Drew and Scott stood in the outfield as the final batters took their cuts.

"Not much of a practice," Drew observed.

"Yeah," Scott said, looking around the field. "I don't know what's going on."

"Me neither," said Drew, looking straight at Scott. "But maybe it's time for the coach to chew these guys out."

Sam Finch lofted a lazy fly ball to short, center field. Scott drifted back a few steps, reached up and caught it in the webbing of his glove. "All right!" he shouted. "Everybody in."

The team gathered quietly. Scott stood before them with his arms crossed.

"Listen," Scott started. "We gotta start practicing harder than this or we're gonna lose all of our games."

Some of the Tigers looked down and scraped the dirt with their shoes.

Scott continued. "Remember, you play the way you practice. You gotta show some hustle. You gotta..."

"Who made you boss?" Danny asked, raising his voice above Scott's.

"What do you mean?" Scott asked, a bit surprised. "I'm the coach. I thought we agreed on that."

"Well, you better start acting like a coach," Danny snapped back. "We've lost every game so far and we keep going out with the same lineup. Don't you think we should try something different?"

"Like what?" Scott demanded.

"I don't know," Danny said. "But I'd like to play somewhere other than catcher."

"Danny, you're our best catcher!" Drew blurted out.

"I'm not the only one!" Danny shouted back.

"I'll catch," Nick said.

40

"Who made you boss?"

Then a chorus of requests burst forth.

"Hey, can I play infield?" Brendan shouted.

"Can I pitch?" Peter asked.

"Can I play shortstop?" asked Max.

"Wait a minute, wait a minute!" Fran shouted above all the others, holding the ball high over her head. "We can't all talk at once. The kid with the ball talks." Fran flipped the ball to Maggie.

Maggie hesitated, then said, "I think we should get a chance to play different positions. And maybe kids like Benny and Brendan should play more."

"Maybe if they..." Drew started to say.

"You don't have the ball," Fran reminded Drew.

Maggie tossed Drew the ball.

"Maybe if they practiced more, they could play more," Drew said.

"Give me the ball, Drew," said Scott. Drew tossed it over to him. "It's tough to have kids play positions in games that they haven't played in practice," Scott explained.

"Hey," said Nick, raising his hand for the ball. "Why don't we practice more? We don't have to wait for Mr. Skelly now. Heck, we could practice every day."

The Tigers nodded their heads. "We could practice every day right after school," Max suggested. "Nobody is using the field then."

Scott glanced at Drew. "It's all right by me," he said. "How about 3:30 to 4:30 every day after school? We'll start tomorrow."

The Tigers gave out a loud cheer. It was the most noise the team had made for a long time. The kids wandered off, leaving Scott, Drew, and Fran to gather the equipment into the brown canvas bag.

"How do you like that?" Drew asked as he tossed a baseball like a jump shot into the bag. "The kids probably think Brain should play shortstop."

"It's more fun if you get to play more positions," Fran said.

"The best kids should play!" Drew said, a little too loudly.

"It's hard to get better if you don't get a chance," Fran answered just as loudly.

"Take it easy," Scott said softly. "We got enough problems on this team without you guys fighting." Scott took a last look around the field. "You guys forget a mitt?" he asked, pointing to a baseball glove in the dugout dirt.

Scott walked over and picked up the glove. The name Benjamin P. Myles was neatly printed along the glove's thumb.

"Whose is it?" Fran asked.

"Benny's," said Scott.

"Just like the Brain to forget his glove," Drew grumbled. "I bet he didn't forget his books. Let's see it." Scott tossed Drew the glove.

"Fran," Scott said, "why don't you take the bag to my house and I'll take Brain his glove."

Drew laughed and said, "Benjamin P. Myles. Man, the Brain must be the only kid in America who puts his middle initial on his glove."

"Wonder what the P stands for," Fran said.

Drew flipped the glove to Scott. "Pathetic," he said.

EIGHT

Scott stood at the Myleses' front door with Benny's glove in his hand. Mrs. Myles answered the bell in a business suit and stocking feet.

"Hi, I'm Scott Hudson. Benny forgot his glove and…"

"Oh, you're coaching the team. Come in. Come in," Mrs. Myles said. She turned her head and shouted up the stairs, "Benjamin!"

"I'm sorry Benjamin's dad and I haven't been able to attend any of the games," she said.

Scott didn't know what to say so he just said, "That's okay. You didn't miss much."

"Benjamin!" Mrs. Myles called again. "He must be on the computer. Benjamin just loves the computer. Why don't you go ahead upstairs?"

Scott started upstairs carrying the glove. Sure enough, he found Benny sitting at the computer tapping away on the keys.

"Hey, Brain," said Scott. "You forgot your glove."

Benny turned, a bit startled. Scott held up the glove.

"Oh yeah, thanks," Benny said and turned back to the computer.

"What are you doing?" Scott asked. "Homework?"

"No, statistics."

"What statistics?"

"The team statistics."

"Really? Can I take a look?"

Scott walked over to the computer. He looked over Benny's shoulder and studied the numbers.

PITCHER	IP	TP	S	B	PCT	R	RA
Drew	16	342	181	161	.529	19	7.12
Scott	11	231	129	102	.558	7	3.82
Nick	1	19	8	11	.421	2	12.00

"What are these?" Scott asked.

"The pitching statistics so far this year," Benny said.

"IP, that's Innings Pitched, right? But what's TP stand for?" Scott asked.

"Total Pitches," Benny explained in his teacher voice. "That's followed by strikes—S;

46

balls pitched—B; and the percentage of pitches that are strikes—PCT.

"R is for runs scored by the other team, right? But what's RA?" asked Scott.

"That's the average number of runs in a game that the other team gets when you pitch."

"My RA is 3.82. So if I pitched a whole game, the other team would get three or four runs. That's pretty good," said Scott.

"It's not bad," Benny said flatly. "But take a look at this."

Benny tapped a few keys and a new set of numbers appeared.

```
Inning          1  2  3  4  5  6
Opponents' runs 3  1  2  7  9  6  28(Total)
```

"What's this?"

"That's the scoring of the other teams against us, broken down by inning. Notice anything?"

"Sure," Scott said. "They're scoring almost all of their runs in the late innings."

Benny nodded. "That's right."

"What do you think we should do?"

"Simple," Benny said. "You shouldn't pitch

for an entire game. You're getting tired and giving up runs in the last innings. Same thing with Drew. You guys should each pitch only three innings a game."

Scott kept studying the numbers on the screen. "Got anything else?" he asked.

"Sure." Benny tapped some more keys and some more numbers appeared.

PLAYER	AB	R	H	K	BB	BA	OBP
Max	20	1	5	3	0	.250	.250
Nick	19	2	5	3	2	.263	.333
Drew	18	3	8	2	2	.444	.500
Danny	17	3	6	5	3	.353	.450
Scott	17	1	6	3	2	.353	.421
Fran	15	1	4	4	3	.266	.388
Maggie	9	2	3	1	7	.333	.625
Peter	12	0	2	5	0	.166	.166
Sam	9	0	1	4	3	.111	.333
Eric	10	0	2	5	0	.200	.200
Brendan	6	0	1	3	0	.166	.166
Michael	9	0	2	2	1	.222	.300
Benny	5	0	0	3	1	.000	.166
Totals	166	13	45	43	24	.271	.363

AB = at bats (how many times a batter was up); R = runs; H = hits; K = strike outs; BB = base on balls (walks); BA = batting average; OBP = on base percentage (how often the batter gets on base with hits or walks).

Scott leaned closer to the computer. "What are these?"

"Batting statistics."

"I know BA is batting average, but what is OBP?"

"On Base Percentage," Benny answered. "It shows how often someone gets on base."

"You mean by getting hits?"

"Yes, and by getting walks. You know you're always saying, 'A walk is as good as a hit.' Well, on base percentage gives a player credit for walks. Batting averages don't."

"Boy, Maggie's got a great OBP," Scott observed.

"That's why she should be the leadoff hitter," Benny said.

"But Max has more hits," Scott protested.

"But Max doesn't get any walks," Benny said, pointing at the column BB (for base on balls). "You want someone at the top of the lineup to get on base. It doesn't matter how. Besides, Maggie's one of the fastest runners on the team."

"Can you print this stuff out for me?" Scott asked.

"No problem." With a few clicks the

*He looked over Benny's shoulder and
studied the numbers.*

printer started to hum and within seconds the Tigers stats started to roll out.

Scott picked up the stats and realized that he was still holding Benny's glove.

"Here's your glove," he said, tossing the mitt to Benny. "Hey, what does the P stand for?"

"Nothing," Benny said, looking away. "My mom wrote that. I hate my middle name."

"Come on, tell me. I won't tell anybody."

"Promise?" Benny eyed Scott with suspicion.

"Promise."

"I don't know."

"Come on, tell me."

"All right...Peaches."

"Peaches? Like the fruit?" Scott blurted out. "What kind of name is that?"

"I told you it was dumb. It's an old family name. I really don't need another nickname so forget I told you."

"Don't worry," Scott said as he turned to leave. "I'll keep your secret."

Scott stopped at the bedroom door and held up the stats.

"Hey, thanks for the stats," he said.

"Don't tell the team that I'm keeping stats,

okay? They'll think it's weird," said Benny.

"They won't think it's weird," Scott protested.

"Drew will," Benny said.

"Yeah, you're probably right," Scott answered. "Well, see you tomorrow at practice...Benny."

NINE

Scott sat in the dugout before the Expos game and looked at the Tigers lineup one more time. He tapped the eraser end of his pencil against the paper, tempted to change the column of names. Finally, he stood up and called, "Bring it in, everybody."

The Tigers gathered around. Scott took a deep breath and said, "Listen up. I'm gonna make some changes. We're up first, so here's the lineup: Maggie's leading off today and playing second."

Scott could feel the team stirring but he continued. "Nick's gonna catch and hit second. Drew's pitching. Danny will start at first and hit cleanup. I'm at short. Max, you're in left batting sixth. Fran's at third. Peter's not here, so Eric will start in center. Benny's in right batting ninth. All right, let's get off to a good start and win one!"

Scott stood at the edge of the dugout as the first Tiger batters picked out their favorite bats and helmets.

"Come on, Maggie!" Scott shouted as Maggie stepped to the plate. "Look 'em over. Walk's as good as a hit."

Drew stood with his hat and batting helmet next to Scott. "What gives?" he asked in a half whisper. "Why am I pitching today? I pitched last game."

"Don't worry. I'm gonna pitch the last three innings," Scott said.

Drew's face twisted into a question mark.

"Just give it your best shot for three innings, okay?" Scott said, turning back to the game. "Come on, Maggie, be a hitter."

"And what's the deal with Maggie leading off?" Drew asked.

"I just figured we better do something different," Scott said, smiling and looking toward Benny. But Benny didn't see the smile. He was scribbling in his notebook as Maggie fouled off a pitch. "Straighten it out, Maggie!" Scott shouted.

"I hope you know what you're doing, Coach," Drew said as he took a practice swing.

The new lineup looked good as Maggie worked a walk to lead off the inning. Nick hit a hard grounder that the Expos shortstop juggled. Maggie slid into second base just before the throw. The Tigers had runners on first and second. No outs.

Drew hit a pop-up that was caught in short, center field. But Danny and Scott both banged out clutch singles to give the Tigers a 2–0 lead.

Drew took the mound. He breezed through the first two innings holding the Expos to one hit. In the bottom of the third inning, with the Tigers still leading 2–0, the Expos batter smacked a two-out single into center field.

"Come on, Drew," Scott chattered from shortstop. "One more out. Bear down, buddy."

The next Expos batter lofted a lazy fly ball to right field. Benny took a couple of nervous steps to his left and held up his glove. The ball plunked against the heel of Benny's glove and dropped to the grass.

"Get it in!" Scott shouted to Benny. The Tigers right fielder tossed the ball to Scott but it was too late to catch the speeding Expos runner at the plate. The Tigers led 2–1.

Drew struck out the next Expos batter with

55

three angry fastballs.

Scott shouted encouragement as the Tigers hustled off the field. "Eric. Then Brendan's hitting for Benny. Then the top of the order. We're gonna need more runs."

Drew looked down the bench to Benny writing in his notebook. "Be sure to put down an error for the right fielder, Brain!" Drew shouted. "Let's try playing baseball instead of just watching it."

"Cut it out, Drew. Believe me, we need Benny," Scott said angrily to his friend. "Now let's get the run back."

The Tigers rallied in the top of the fourth inning. Brendan, Maggie, and Drew loaded up the bases with a walk and two singles.

Scott knew a big moment in the game had come when Danny stepped to the plate. *Bases loaded, two outs, one-run lead,* Scott thought, as he stood at the on-deck circle rubbing his bat nervously.

"Come on, Danny, be a sticker. Ducks on the pond!" shouted Scott.

Danny drilled a line shot to left center field. The Expos left fielder raced over and leaped. The ball whizzed by his outstretched

Danny drilled a line shot to left center field.

glove and bounced to the wall.

The Tiger bench exploded in cheers as three Tigers sprinted around the bases and crossed home plate.

"All right, Danny! Big stick!"

"Three runs batted in. Let's get some more!"

The Tigers added another run in the later innings, but it hardly mattered. Scott pitched three solid innings and the Tigers won for the first time that season, 6–1.

After the last out, the team swarmed around Scott chanting, "Game ball, game ball, game ball." Scott held up a battered baseball for silence.

"Everybody played great today but this can only go to one guy. Danny's double broke the game open," Scott said, tossing the ball to Danny as the Tigers whooped and hollered.

The team left happy. Smiling, Scott gathered the equipment into the big brown bag. Slinging the heavy bag onto his back, Scott walked over to Benny who was sitting alone on the grandstand studying his notebook.

"Got today's pitching stats?" Scott asked.

"Yeah, want to take a look?"

Scott studied the neat columns of figures.

Pitcher	Inning	Strikes	Balls	Batters	Runs
Drew	1st	𝄇𝄇𝄇 ⑫	𝄇 ⑤	④	0
	2nd	𝄇𝄇 ⑩	𝄇 ⑧	④	0
	3rd	𝄇𝄇𝄇 ⑬	𝄇𝄇 ⑫	⑤	1
	Totals	35	25	13	1
Scott					
	4th	𝄇 ⑦	③	③	0
	5th	𝄇𝄇 ⑫	𝄇𝄇 ⑩	⑤	0
	6th	𝄇𝄇𝄇 ⑭	𝄇𝄇 ⑪	⑤	0
	Totals	33	24	13	0

"They look pretty good," Scott said, still smiling.

Benny pointed to the paper. "Notice your first inning was a lot stronger then Drew's last. He was starting to get tired."

Scott nodded. "Looks like you're a pretty good coach, Peaches," he winked.

"Don't call me Peaches, okay?"

"Okay, Benny."

TEN

Three weeks later, Scott, Drew, and Fran blew through the door of the Hudsons' house and threw their baseball gloves on a chair.

"Is that you, Scott?" called Scott's father from the kitchen.

"Yeah, Dad."

"How was practice?"

"Great! The team is getting better all the time."

"You should be. You guys are practicing almost every day. Do you have much home-work tonight?"

"Not much. I did most of it in school. Drew, Fran, and I are going upstairs, okay?"

"Fine with me. We'll eat when Mom gets home from work. I'm going to make ham-burgers."

"Right, Dad," Scott called as he scrambled up the stairs.

The three friends flew into Scott's bedroom. Drew grabbed a small ball and tossed a
quick jump shot at the miniature hoop hang-
ing on the closet door. *Swish.*

"Okay. What did you want to show us?"
Drew asked.

"Not so fast. First look at this," Scott said as
he handed Drew and Fran the Tigers schedule.
Drew and Fran glanced down the columns.

Apr 13	1:00 P.M.	Expos	L 5-4
Apr 17	6:30 P.M.	Braves	L 3-2
Apr 20	11:00 A.M.	Cubs	L 5-3
Apr 23	6:30 P.M.	Yankees	L 4-2
Apr 27	3:00 P.M.	Red Sox	L 11-2
May 1	6:30 P.M.	Expos	W 6-1
May 4	11:00 A.M.	Braves	W 4-3
May 7	6:30 P.M.	Cubs	L 4-0
May 10	6:30 P.M.	Yankees	W 5-4
May 14	6:30 P.M.	Red Sox	L 8-1
May 18	3:00 P.M.	Expos	W 2-0
May 23	6:30 P.M.	Braves	W 10-3
May 25	1:00 P.M.	Cubs	W 5-2
May 29	6:30 P.M.	Yankees	
June 1	3:00 P.M.	Red Sox	

"We still got a shot at a winning season,
don't you think?" Scott asked.

"Maybe," said Fran.

"Fat chance," said Drew, tapping the schedule. "We got the Yanks and the Red Sox left, and we'd have to win both games. Eddie Wilson of the Red Sox is the best hitter in town. And the only guys hitting in our team are you, me, and Danny."

"Come on, Drew," said Fran. "What about Maggie and me? We're no slouches."

"Fran's right," Scott said. "Here. This is what I wanted to show you." Scott opened a desk drawer and pulled out a piece of paper and handed it to Drew.

"What's this?" Drew asked.

"The team batting statistics after 13 games."

Drew studied them as Fran looked over his shoulder.

"What's OBP?" Drew asked.

"On Base Percentage—how often a batter gets on base. And walks count," said Scott.

Fran pointed at the paper. "Hey, Maggie's got the best OBP on the team."

"You're right, Fran," said Drew, turning a little red.

"That's why Maggie's the leadoff hitter," Scott said, sounding a bit like Benny.

Fran looked at Scott. "Did you do these stats?" she asked.

	AB	R	H	K	BB	BA	OBP
Max	42	3	11	9	2	.262	.295
Nick	45	6	13	7	6	.289	.373
Drew	49	8	20	5	5	.408	.463
Danny	44	7	17	10	7	.386	.471
Scott	45	5	15	7	6	.333	.412
Fran	42	4	13	8	8	.310	.420
Maggie	29	9	11	3	17	.379	.608
Peter	33	1	7	13	2	.212	.257
Sam	25	1	5	10	4	.200	.310
Eric	23	1	6	9	1	.261	.292
Brendan	19	1	5	6	2	.263	.333
Michael	21	0	6	6	2	.286	.348
Benny	12	0	1	7	3	.083	.266
Totals	429	46	130	100	65	.303	.395

"No."

"Your dad?"

Scott shook his head.

"Who then?"

"Benny," Scott said matter-of-factly.

"Benny!" said Drew. "So that's what the Brain's been doing with all the stuff he writes in his notebooks." Then Drew laughed, pointing at the paper. "The Brain does a lot better job keeping the stats than he does playing the game. You know who is the worst hitter? Benjamin P. Myles," said Drew. "He's 1 for 12."

"Give Benny a break, Drew," Scott said. "He's getting better, especially in the field. And his stats have really helped the team. Face it, you couldn't do the stats."

"What do you mean?" Drew asked, sounding hurt. "I got a B in math on my last report card. I could keep the stats."

"You know what I mean," Scott said. "We'd be lost without Benny's brain power."

"Yeah, maybe," Drew said, and he quickly changed the subject. "Hey, did you ever find out what the P stands for in Brain's name?" he asked.

"Oh yeah, it stands for..." Scott stopped, remembering his promise.

"Come on, what's it stand for?" Drew pressed.

"Nah...I...ah...promised Benny I wouldn't tell anyone."

"Come on, we're buddies."

Scott shook his head.

"Come on, tell. Fran and I won't blab it to anybody," Drew said.

"All right," Scott said impatiently. "It's Peaches."

"Peaches!" Fran and Drew blurted out at the same time.

"Come on, you guys, and don't tell anybody," Scott pleaded. "And don't tell anybody that Benny's keeping stats. He doesn't want anybody to know."

"I can see why he doesn't want anybody knowing his middle name," said Fran. "I won't tell anybody."

Fran and Scott then looked over at Drew.

"Don't worry!" Drew said. "I can keep a secret."

ELEVEN

Scott stood on the pitcher's mound rubbing the baseball and eyeing the Yankee runners at first and second bases. He glanced over his shoulder to the scoreboard behind the center-field fence. The Yankees led 5–2 in the top of the third.

"Come on, Scottie," Fran called from third base. "One more out. No batter, no batter."

Scott hurled a hard pitch toward the outside corner of the plate. The Yankee batter knocked a hard hopper to the right side of the infield. Danny, who was playing first base, dove to his right and knocked the ball down.

In a flash, Scott dashed off the mound to cover first base. Scrambling to his knees, Danny tossed the ball toward first. Racing to first, Scott reached out, caught the ball, and touched the bag a split second before the runner.

"Out!" the umpire cried.

The Tigers were out of the inning!

"Listen up!" Scott shouted as the Tigers got ready to hit in the bottom of the third inning. "Next inning, Drew's pitching and I'm playing short. Danny and Nick switch. Benny's in right for Sam. Brendan, you're in left for Peter. Let's get some runs."

The Tigers didn't score and neither did the Yankees. In the bottom of the fourth, Danny and Scott led with a pair of singles.

"Come on, Fran!" Scott shouted from first base. "Big stick."

Fran watched two pitches go by and then scorched a line drive to center field. Scott and Danny sprinted around the bases as the ball flew over the surprised Yankee center fielder. The Tigers had cut the lead to 5–4.

The Tigers were still trailing by one run when they came to bat in the bottom of the sixth and final inning.

"Last licks," Scott cried. "Fran, Max, Brendan, Benny, and then the top of the order."

"Let's put on our rally caps!" Drew shouted as he walked down the Tigers bench with his hat on backwards. As he walked by, all of the

Tigers turned their hats around.

"Come on, Fran, get it going. Rally time!"

The Tigers rally started slowly when Fran grounded out to the pitcher. Max popped a weak single to right field. Brendan struck out swinging.

The Tigers hopes for a winning season were down to the last out. *Two outs, runner on first*, Scott thought, *and the Tigers worst hitter, Benjamin P. Myles, coming to bat.*

Drew grabbed Scott by the arm. "Scott, you gotta pinch-hit Eric for the Brain!"

Scott looked down the bench at Eric, who was chewing gum and swinging his legs back and forth. "He's not so hot either," whispered Scott.

"Give Benny a chance," said Fran. "He's been hitting better in practice."

"He's only gotten one hit in a game," Drew snapped at Fran.

"He's due for another!" Fran yelled back.

"Cut it out guys. Let him hit," Scott said as he turned his eyes toward Benny and held his breath.

"Oh, man..." Drew groaned, falling back against the dugout wall.

Benny tapped the plate with his bat and assumed his stance.

"Come on, Benny," Fran cheered. "Only takes one. Be a hitter."

The first pitch whistled by him. Strike one.

"Yeah, come on, Brain!" Drew shouted. "Hit that peach."

Scott turned to Drew with angry eyes. "Cut it out!" he said.

The second pitch skipped low. Ball one.

"What did I do?" Drew asked.

"You know what you did," said Fran. "Stop being a jerk."

Benny swung and missed the next pitch. One ball, two strikes.

"You think *I'm* being a jerk?" asked Drew. "I'm not the one putting up the worst hitter on the team for the most important at bat in the season!"

The three friends looked out to home plate without much hope. On the next pitch, Benny took a full swing but only connected with the top part of the ball, sending it dribbling down toward third base. Benny sprinted to first with a single on the infield grass just inside the foul line.

The Tigers bench filled with cheers.

"All right!" Fran shouted. "I told you Benny was due for a hit!"

"Yeah, a lucky hit," Scott said as he let out his breath in a whoosh.

"All right, Brain!" Drew shouted. "Way to hit that..." Drew hesitated and glanced at Scott and Fran, "that apple."

Maggie walked to load up the bases. The Tigers were on their feet.

"Come on, Nick. Just meet it."

"Two outs," Scott reminded the runners. "Go on anything."

The Tiger runners were off when Nick ripped a line drive to left field. Max made it easily to home and Benny wheeled around third base, racing the left fielder's throw to the plate. The ball bounced just in front of the Yankee catcher and skidded away as Benny slid across the plate in a spray of dirt.

The Tigers had won 6–5!

The whole team surrounded Benny at home plate, happily slapping his back and helmet. Then, above all the noise and joy came Drew's voice. "All right, Peaches!" he shouted.

Inside the circle of happy teammates,

Benny slid across the plate in a spray of dirt.

Benny's head jerked back in surprise. Benny looked at Drew, then to Scott. Benny and Scott's eyes met for a moment. Scott looked away and then toward Drew and just shook his head.

Fran just stood there frozen, not saying a word.

As the excitement died down, Fran loosened up and Scott grabbed the game ball. The Tigers gathered around Scott. Everyone was excited about the big win. "Quiet down. I've got the ball so I'm the only one who can talk, remember," said Scott. "That was a great game. We had a lot of heroes. But I think the game ball should go to..." Scott searched the circle of players for Benny, but Benny was gone. Past the players, Scott saw Benny walking quickly away.

Scott paused. "Fran," he said finally, tossing the ball to the surprised third sacker.

The team cheered and slowly wandered away. Scott and Fran stayed behind, putting the equipment in the big brown bag.

"I didn't deserve the game ball," Fran said, picking up a batting helmet from behind the backstop. "Benny deserved it. Or maybe Nick.

They got the big hits. Poor Benny. I bet he's pretty upset."

"Why did Drew have to call him Peaches?" said Scott as he slammed a bat into the bag. "Now he knows I told Drew his secret."

Fran handed the batting helmet to Scott and said, "Well, I guess you'll just have to say you're sorry," she said.

"I guess so," Scott answered.

Fran flipped Scott the game ball. "Here," she said. "Give this to Benny when you talk to him. Maybe it will help say you're sorry."

TWELVE

"I'm not sure where Benjamin is," Mrs. Myles said to Scott as he stood at the Myleses' front door the next evening. "He went out on his bike about twenty minutes ago."

"Do you know where he went?"

Mrs. Myles thought for a moment. "He's been going down to the school a lot lately to practice catching fly balls. He throws the ball against the high brick wall in the back," she said, and then paused. "Wait a minute. He didn't take his glove with him. He took his notebook," she said, mostly to herself. "You know what, Scott? I bet he's gone to the baseball field to watch a game. Try there."

"Okay. Thanks, Mrs. Myles," Scott said and he hopped on his bicycle and pedaled toward the field. Along the way, he thought of what he would say to Benny. Scott had wanted to apologize to Benny at school but he hadn't seen him.

Scott stopped on the small hill overlooking the baseball field. He saw Benny sitting alone on a corner of the small grandstand with a notebook on his lap. Scott parked his bike and walked slowly to the stands, plopping himself on the row below Benny. "Hey, Benny," he said, trying to sound cheerful.

"Oh, hi," he said. Benny looked up from his notebook for just a second, then he made a mark in it, and looked back at the game.

Scott figured he should get it over with. "Listen," he said. "I'm sorry about the whole Peaches thing with Drew. I shouldn't have told him."

"I asked you not to," Benny said, still watching the game.

"Yeah, I know," said Scott. "But...well...I'm sorry."

Benny kept looking out at the game as he spoke. "I was just getting used to the kids calling me Brain. I don't need another nickname, you know. And why did you tell Drew? He's the worst."

"He's not so bad," Scott said.

"Not to you," said Benny, "because you're good at sports."

Scott reached into his pants pocket and pulled out the game ball. "You left the last game too early," Scott said. "I was gonna give you the game ball."

Benny looked at the ball. "Give it to somebody else," he said, turning his attention to the game. "I don't want your game ball."

"You know, Benny, you're really our Most Valuable Player. I mean the stats you've been keeping turned our club around," said Scott. "I don't think the other guys would think it's weird if they knew you were keeping them."

"Maybe not," said Benny, still scribbling away in his notebook.

"What are you doing?" Scott asked, pointing to the notebook.

"Keeping the stats on the Red Sox," Benny answered.

"You keep stats on the other teams?"

"Yeah."

"Hey, Eddie Wilson is coming up. I bet he hits a home run," said Scott.

"The odds against that are about 12 to 1," Benny said. "But I will bet that he hits it to the right side of the field."

"Really?"

"Listen," he said. "I'm sorry about the whole
Peaches thing with Drew."

"He hits it there about nine out of ten times."

Just then, Wilson lashed a line drive between the center fielder and right fielder for a triple.

"See, what did I tell you?" said Benny. He made a quick mark in his notebook.

"So what do you think we should do when Eddie comes to bat against us on Saturday?" Scott asked.

"Use the Williams shift," Benny answered.

"What's that?"

"That's what Lou Boudreau used against Hall of Famer Ted Williams about fifty years ago."

"Lou Boudreau," Scott remembered. "He was the player-coach you mentioned at the board meeting, wasn't he?"

"Right."

"Well, what's the Williams shift?"

Benny flipped over some pages in his notebook and began to draw a diagram of a baseball diamond. When he finished his drawing he tore out the page and handed it to Scott.

"What if Eddie hits it to left field?" Scott asked.

"He won't."

"What if he sees what we're doing and tries to hit to the left?"

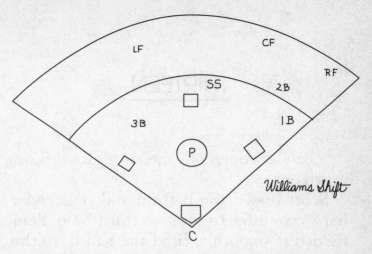

Williams Shift

"He'll be trying to do something he usually doesn't do. That helps us."

"What if he bunts?"

"Wouldn't you like Eddie Wilson to bunt instead of trying to hit a home run?"

Scott looked at the diagram for a while. "Can I keep this?" he asked.

"Sure."

Scott tucked the paper into his pocket and started to leave.

"Thanks, Benny," said Scott. "Listen, I'm sorry about telling Drew."

"You should be," Benny said flatly. Then he scribbled something in his notebook.

THIRTEEN

"Okay, last one, Fran, then bring it in," Scott called out.

Scott tossed the ball up and smacked a hard grounder to Fran at third base. Fran fielded it smoothly, fired the ball in to the catcher, and jogged off the field.

Scott continued to hit grounders around the practice field. Each Tiger fielder gathered the ball in, threw to home plate, and jogged off the field. The last ball went to Benny in right field.

"Come on, Benny, get the ball to Danny. Step into it," Scott said.

Benny charged in, scooped up the grounder, and threw it hard. The ball bounced twice before it reached Danny's catcher's mitt, but it got there. Danny flipped the ball to Scott.

"Benny's looking a lot better in the out-field," Danny said as he watched Benny trot in toward home plate.

Benny and Danny walked over to the circle of Tigers near the dugout.

Scott quickly got down to business. "All right. Quiet. I've got the ball so I get to talk," said Scott, holding the ball high over his head. "We're playing the Red Sox tomorrow. We'll finish with a winning record if we can beat them. I know they beat us bad before, but I think we're a lot better now."

Drew motioned for the ball and Scott tossed it to him.

"Can we go and let the air out of Eddie Wilson's bike tires or something?" joked Drew. "He's been killing us."

The team laughed as Scott caught the ball from Drew.

"I think we've got a plan that might help."

Scott tossed the ball to Benny who was standing off to the side. "Tell the team about your plan, Benny," Scott said.

"Me?" asked Benny, almost dropping the ball.

"Yeah, you came up with it," said Scott.

"All right," said Benny, with the ball now firmly in his grip. "It's pretty simple. Eddie's a left-handed batter who pulls the ball. In fact, he hits the ball to the right side of the field about 90 percent of the time."

"How do you know that?" Nick asked.

"I, uh, um, I...I keep statistics on all the teams," Benny said.

"All the teams? What for?" Drew asked.

"Quiet!" Fran shouted. "Benny's got the ball. Let him finish."

Benny continued. "So I figured we should shift fielders over toward right field. We would only leave Fran at third and the left fielder on the left side, and even they would move way over."

"That's crazy!" said Drew, looking around at his teammates. Most of them were nodding their heads and laughing.

"It worked against Ted Williams," Scott said. "And he was a Hall of Famer."

"What if Eddie hits to the left?" Drew asked.

"He almost never does," Scott said.

"What if he bunts?" Drew asked.

"Great! I'd rather him bunt than hit the ball out of the park!" said Scott as he and Benny exchanged smiles.

"What if he does hit it out of the park?" Drew asked.

"Then it won't matter where we put the fielders," Benny said. This time the team was laughing at Drew.

"Come on, it's worth a try," Fran said. "We can't do much worse. The Red Sox have been killing us!"

"Yeah, come on. Let's give it a shot," Scott said. "The regular starters take the field. I'll try to hit a few by you."

The Tigers trotted out to their positions. "Move back, Maggie," said Scott, pointing with his bat. "And Drew, you should be a step or two to the right of second base. Fran, swing around to shortstop."

"Hey!" Drew shouted in from second base. "I got an idea. Maybe we should switch the right and left fielder, so Max is playing right field against Eddie."

Scott knew that Max was their best out-fielder. He looked at Benny on the sidelines. Benny nodded. "He's right. The percentages are better with Max in right."

"All right," Scott shouted. "Max play right. Sam play left in the shift."

After the shift was in place, Scott tried to smash a few shots past the bunched fielders.

The Tigers gobbled them up with glee. After a while, Scott called an end to the practice.

The kids wandered away from practice. But Drew hung around and helped Scott pick up the equipment.

"What do you think of the shift?" Scott asked.

"It seems okay," Drew said with a shrug. Then he smiled. "But maybe we should put someone over the right field fence when Eddie comes to bat. That's where the ball will be headed."

FOURTEEN

"Play ball!" the umpire shouted, pulling down his mask and motioning Scott to pitch.

Scott turned to check his fielders. Then he fired a fastball to start the Tigers final game of the season.

The Red Sox leadoff hitter topped a slow roller to third. Fran rushed in, scooped up the ball, and threw to first, all in one motion. One out.

The second Red Sox batter popped a weak fly ball to center field. "I got it!" called Peter. Two outs.

Eddie Wilson stepped to the plate. Scott held up his hands and called, "Time." Turning to the fielders, Scott waved his teammates into their shift positions. Sam raced over to left field and Max dashed to right field. As Scott turned to face the star Red Sox slugger, Mr. Robinson, the Red Sox coach, charged out to the umpire. "Hey, ump," he called out. "They can't do that, can they? Bunching the kids together like that?"

Scott joined the umpire and Mr. Robinson in front of home plate. "Well, coach," the umpire said, holding his mask and scratching his head. "I don't know. I can't say as I've seen it before."

"It's the Williams shift," Scott said. "Lou Boudreau used it against Ted Williams about fifty years ago."

The umpire nodded. "I think he's right. Teams today do something like it against some of the big hitters."

"Yeah, but they can't change their left and right fielders, can they?" said Mr. Robinson.

The umpire pulled a notebook from his back pocket and thumbed through the pages. "I don't see anything against it," he said shaking his head. "The rule book just says that you gotta have at least three outfielders. And they got three outfielders. They're in funny places but they are in the outfield."

Mr. Robinson stood with his hands on his hips for a long moment. Then he turned and walked back to the bench.

"Play ball!" the umpire shouted.

Scott stood on the mound and concentrated on pitching again. At the plate, Eddie Wilson eyed the Tigers fielders and looked confused.

Scott threw the first pitch high. Ball one. Scott blazed the second pitch right down the middle, but Eddie let it go by. Strike!

Scott put a little extra on the next pitch. Eddie Wilson swung and scorched a screaming line drive to right center-field. Peter was standing in the perfect position; the ball landed smack in his glove.

The shift had worked!

The game settled into a surprisingly close struggle. The Red Sox scored a run in the top of the second inning, but the Tigers got the run back in the bottom of the third when Maggie scored on a double by Danny. So when Scott handed the ball to Drew to pitch the last three innings, the game was tied, 1–1.

Eddie Wilson led off the top of the fourth inning. The Tigers went into the shift behind Drew. The Tiger pitcher got two quick strikes on the Red Sox slugger.

Standing in back of second base, Scott could see that Eddie was trying to push the ball to the left but could not do it. After two pitches in the dirt, Drew put one right across the heart of the plate. Eddie lashed a liner out toward second base. Scott took one quick step and leaped. The ball whistled by Scott's outstretched glove. Scott turned to watch the ball take a crazy hop on the outfield grass over Peter's glove and roll to the wall.

Running hard, Eddie Wilson made it to third base with a leadoff triple. He trotted home on a long fly ball by the Red Sox cleanup hitter. The Red Sox led 2–1.

"Come on, let's get it back," Scott said as the Tigers prepared to bat in the bottom of the fourth inning. Drew threw his glove against the bench.

"Why don't we ditch this stupid shift thing, Scott?" he said. "It's not working."

"What do you mean?" Scott asked.

"He's batting .500!" Drew shouted.

Benny put down his notebook and scooted down the bench to where Scott and Drew were talking. "The shift isn't going to stop him every time," Benny explained. "It just makes it harder for him to get a hit. It is just playing percentages."

Drew turned on Benny. "We're not playing percentages out here, Brain. We're playing baseball!" Drew snapped. "And this shift thing isn't working."

"Chill out, both of you," Scott ordered. "We're going to stick with the shift. Benny, you're going into right field next inning. Let's concentrate on getting some runs."

The Tigers did not score in the bottom of the fourth inning. Drew set the Red Sox down in order in the top of the fifth. So the Tigers still trailed by one run when they came to bat in the bottom of the fifth inning.

"Benny, you're up!" Scott shouted. "Then the top of the order. Look them over. We need base runners."

"Come on, guys, rally caps!" Drew called out, turning his Tigers hat backwards on his head.

The rally started slowly. Benny struck out swinging. Maggie grounded out to first. But Nick kept his teammates' hopes alive with a sharp single.

Drew dug in at the plate.

"Come on, Drew. Keep it going."

"Two-out rally!"

Drew jumped on the first pitch and sent a shot to right center field. Nick sprinted to third and Drew slid into second. The Tigers had runners on second and third. Two outs.

"Time!" the umpire called as Mr. Robinson walked slowly to the pitcher's mound. Scott stood in the on-deck circle watching the conference on the mound as he nervously tested his swing.

Mr. Robinson jogged back to the dugout. Danny stepped into the batter's box ready to hit.

"Come on, Danny, be a hitter."

"Just takes one, Danny."

The Red Sox catcher stood up behind the plate and reached out his glove. The Red Sox pitcher lobbed a pitch several feet outside. Ball one.

The Red Sox were walking Danny on purpose. *Of course*, Scott thought, *walking Danny makes perfect sense. Now, the Red Sox can get an out at any base! I'm going to hit with the bases loaded!*

FIFTEEN

Scott's heart pounded as he dug his right foot into the back of the batter's box. He took a deep breath and stared out at the Red Sox pitcher. *Better start thinking like a player and not like a coach,* Scott reminded himself.

The Red Sox pitcher wound up and spun a belt-high fastball across the inside half of the plate. Strike one!

Scott laid off the second pitch that was outside. Ball one.

Scott fouled off the next pitch. One ball, two strikes. Scott was down to his last strike. *Get the bat started*, Scott said to himself.

The Red Sox pitcher fired a hard one to the inside part of the plate. Scott swung and knocked a line drive to left field. As he ran to first base, Scott glanced to his left to see the ball fall in front of the Red Sox outfielders for a hit. Nick and Drew sprinted home. The

Tigers led 3–2!

The chance to add to their lead was cut off when Fran popped up to end the inning.

"Come on, Tigers!" Scott shouted. "Last inning. Let's play good defense."

The team was psyched. The infield was filled with chatter.

"Come on, Drew. Blow it by them!"

"One, two, three, Drew."

"No batter, no batter."

The Red Sox leadoff hitter slapped an easy one-hopper to Drew. The Tigers pitcher lobbed a quick throw to first. One out.

The second Red Sox batter sliced a line shot to left field. Eric juggled the ball just enough to allow the batter to cruise into second base.

Runner on second, one out. And Eddie Wilson was coming up.

Drew held up his hands and called, "Time." He motioned Scott to the mound with his glove. Danny took his catcher's mask off and joined the conference.

"Let's forget the shift," Drew suggested. "Why don't we walk Eddie and set up easy plays at..."

"No!" Scott said, shaking his head. "That

would put the winning run on base. Let's take our chances with Eddie."

"Come on, Drew, you can get him out, " Danny said, pulling his mask down over his face. "Just throw hard."

Drew nodded. "Okay."

Scott looked out at the Tigers fielders.

"Put the shift on," he called.

Eric ran from left field over to right. Benny, who had been playing right field, ran over to be the only fielder on the left side of the outfield. Scott trotted to his position on the first base side of second base.

"Come on, Drew. No batter, no batter."

Drew threw a fastball, high. Ball one.

"Throw strikes, Drew, throw strikes."

The second pitch was a bit inside. Eddie swung and missed.

Scott could see that once again Eddie was trying to push the ball to the left against the shift. Scott edged a few steps over to the left side of the infield.

Drew threw hard for the outside corner.

Crack! Eddie Wilson's smooth swing sent the ball sailing down the left-field line.

But the ball did not have the distance of one

93

of Eddie's homerun drives to right field, and started to fall into the empty space of left field.

"Oh, no!" Scott cried as he watched Benny race to the left-field corner, looking up at the fast-falling ball.

The Red Sox runner at second took off. There seemed no way that Benny would catch the towering fly. But at the last moment, Benny leaped, stretching for the ball like a football receiver. The ball wedged into the webbing of Benny's glove as he tumbled onto the outfield grass.

"What a catch!" Scott yelled, punching his fist into the air.

"Get it to second!" Drew screamed. "Double play!"

Benny sprang to his feet with the ball in his glove. He looked both dazed and thrilled.

"Throw me the ball!" Scott shouted, racing out to left field. The Red Sox runner, already past third base, started scrambling back to second.

Benny lofted a throw over Scott's head.

"Oh, Benny!" Scott groaned, thinking the Tigers chance at a double play was slipping away. But Maggie was ready. She stopped the

*Benny leaped, stretching for the ball
like a football receiver.*

wild throw on the outfield grass in back of second and dashed to the bag. Maggie was one stride ahead of the runner. She pushed her foot hard on the base and threw her arms up in triumph.

"Way to go, Maggie!"

"Great catch, Benny!"

The Tigers had won, 3–2!

After shaking hands with the shocked Red Sox, the Tigers stood outside the dugout celebrating. All together they started chanting: "Game ball! Game ball! Game ball!"

Scott held the ball up for quiet. "I think we all know who's getting this ball," he said, smiling.

"All right, Benny."

"Attaway, Brain."

"Way to go, Peaches."

Scott shot Drew an angry glance.

"I mean Benny. Way to go, Benny," Drew said, smiling at Benny.

Scott held the ball up again. "Benny helped the team all year by keeping the stats, making suggestions, thinking up the shift, and just knowing a lot about baseball."

"Knowing baseball?" Drew blurted out. "How about that catch? That's playing baseball!"

The team cheered as Scott tossed Benny the ball.

The Tigers seemed to drift away more slowly following this last game. Finally, only Drew, Fran, and Benny were left. They helped Scott put the helmets, bats, and memories of another baseball season into the battered brown equipment bag.

"I can't believe it's over," Scott said, tossing a final helmet into the bag.

"I can't believe we did so well," Fran said. "We had a winning season."

Drew pointed his thumb at Benny and laughed. "I can't believe that Benny made that catch."

The kids laughed and looked at Benny. "I can't believe Drew is calling me Benny," he said, flipping the game ball happily in the air.

The End

TURN THE PAGE— THERE'S MORE….

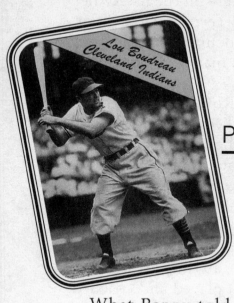

Lou Boudreau
Cleveland Indians

Player Coaches, The Real Story

What Benny told his teammates about player-coaches is true. Years ago, it was fairly common for Major League ball players to take on the added responsibility of coaching their teams. They called these guys player-coaches (or player-managers).

The list of player-coaches includes some of the biggest names in baseball history. Ty Cobb (career batting average of .367), Rogers Hornsby (.358), home-run slugger Mel Ott (511 homers), and pitching great Christy

Mathewson (373 wins) are on the list. Other Hall of Famers like Bill Terry, George Sisler, Joe Cronin, Mickey Cochrane, and Harold Joseph "Pie" Traynor all managed teams during their playing years.

The legendary Babe Ruth wanted to manage the New York Yankees near the end of his playing career, but the owners of the Yankees said no. They thought the "Sultan of Swat" (as Babe Ruth was known) was too undependable to run a baseball team.

Today you don't hear much about player-coaches. Most of them played ball before the 1950s. But in the 1970s, all-time great Frank Robinson (586 homers) played and coached with the Cleveland Indians. Pete Rose, another all-time great (4256 hits), was a player-coach for the Cincinnati Reds in the 1980s.

Probably the greatest single season any player-coach has had in the history of baseball was the season Lou Boudreau (Boo-DRO) had in 1948. Boudreau, a shortstop with the Cleveland Indians, became the team's player-coach in 1942 when he was only twenty-four years old. He was so young that the newspapers sometimes called him "The Boy Manager."

Boudreau wasn't a terrific player-coach right away. In the Indians first six years under Boudreau, they never finished higher than third place in the American League. Things were looking so bad for Boudreau that the Indians almost traded him in 1947.

It's a good thing they didn't—1948 was a magical year for Boudreau. As he put it: "I had angels on my shoulders." Boudreau batted .355 with 18 home runs and 106 runs batted in. He led American League shortstops in double plays and fielding percentage and he was named the American League's Most Valuable Player (MVP).

That year, the Indians—coached by Boudreau—tied the Boston Red Sox for first place in the American League with a record of 96–58. Boudreau smashed two home runs and two singles in an 8–3 victory over the Red Sox in a playoff game. Then, Boudreau led the Indians to the World Series Championship over the Boston Braves in six games.

Imagine if modern-day shortstops Cal Ripken and Barry Larkin, during their MVP years, also coached their teams to the World Championship. That is what Lou Boudreau did in 1948.

Benny was also right that Lou Boudreau is known for the "The Williams Shift." Just like Benny, Boudreau had been keeping notes. He knew that Ted Williams of the Boston Red Sox, a left-handed slugger, hit the ball to the right side of the field 95 percent of the time. So when Ted Williams got up to bat, Boudreau shifted his fielders to the right side of the field. Other major league teams followed Boudreau and started using the shift against Ted Williams.

Did the shift work? Well, yes and no. There were times when Williams tried so hard to blast the ball past the fielders that he did not hit very well. For example, the St. Louis Cardinals used the shift against Williams in the 1946 World Series and the Red Sox star hit only .200 (5 singles in 25 at bats) with no home runs.

But the Williams Shift did not keep Ted Williams from being one of the greatest hitters of his era. In fact, Williams ended his career with .344 batting average and 521 home runs. Because, as Benny found out, no matter where the coach places the fielders, someone has to catch the ball to get the batter out. That's playing baseball.

Acknowledgments

As always, the author would like to thank Scot Mondore at the National Baseball Hall of Fame in Cooperstown, New York. This time, Mr. Mondore dug up interesting information on player-coach Lou Boudreau.

About the Author

One of Fred Bowen's earliest memories is watching the 1957 World Series with his brothers and father on the family's black-and-white television in Marblehead, Massachusetts. Mr. Bowen was four years old.

When he was six years old, he was the batboy for his older brother Rich's Little League team. At nine years old, he played on a team, spending a great deal of time keeping the bench warm. By age eleven, he was a Little League All Star. Mr. Bowen has coached kids' baseball for more than ten years.

Mr. Bowen, author of *T. J.'s Secret Pitch, The Golden Glove, Playoff Dreams, Full Court Fever, Off the Rim, The Final Cut, On the Line,* and *Winners Take All,* lives in Silver Spring, Maryland, with his wife and two children.

Book Four in the
AllStar SportStory Series—
PLAYOFF DREAMS

Brendan is a star player on a team going nowhere. He makes great throws and watches
his teammates drop them. When his team is
at bat, Brendan gets on base, but his teammates don't drive him home. It looks like
Brendan's playoff dreams are never going to
come true—at least not with this team!

When his uncle takes him to a game at
Wrigley Field, an unexpected event and the
story of a legendary Cubs player make
Brendan begin to see his team in a new light.

Follow the team to the exciting end of the
season when Brendan learns what the game
of baseball is all about.

Look for Fred Bowen's

PLAYOFF DREAMS